Emmanuel Guibert

ARiOL

A Beautiful Cow

PAPERCUTZ™

ARIOL Graphic Novels available from PAPERCUTZ™

Graphic Novel #1
"Just a Donkey Like You and Me"

Graphic Novel #2
"Thunder Horse"

Graphic Novel #3
"Happy as a Pig..."

Graphic Novel #4
"A Beautiful Cow"

Graphic Novel #5
"Bizzbilla Hits the Bullseye"

Coming Soon!
Graphic Novel #6
"A Nasty Cat"

ARIOL graphic novels are available for $12.99 only in paperback. Available from booksellers everywhere. You can also order online from www.papercutz.com. Or call 1-800-886-1223, Monday through Friday, 9-5 EST. MC, Visa and AmEx accepted. To order by mail, please add $4.00 for postage and handling for first book ordered, $1.00 for each additional book and make check payable to NBM Publishing. Send to: Papercutz, 160 Broadway, Suite 700, East Wing, New York, NY 10038.

ARIOL graphic novels are also available digitally wherever e-books are sold.

papercutz.com

A Beautiful Cow

To Mr. Nays,
- Emmanuel Guibert

ARiOL

#4 A Beautiful Cow

Emmanuel Guibert - Writer
Marc Boutavant - Artist
Rémi Chaurand - Colorist
Joe Johnson - Translation
Bryan Senka - Lettering
Beth Scorzato - Production Coordinator
Michael Petranek - Associate Editor
Jim Salicrup
Editor-in-Chief

ISBN: 978-1-59707-513-8

Printed in China
August 2014 by New Era Printing, LTD.
Unit C. 8/F Worldwide Centre
123 Chung Tau, Kowloon
Hong Kong

Papercutz books may be purchased for business or promotional use. For information on bulk purchases please contact Macmillan Corporate and Premium Sales Department at (800) 221-7945 x5442.

Distributed by Macmillan
Second Papercutz Printing

ARiOL

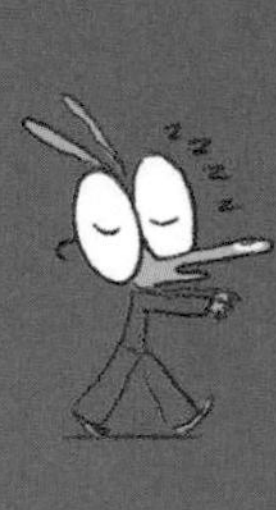

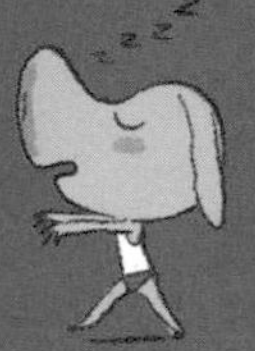

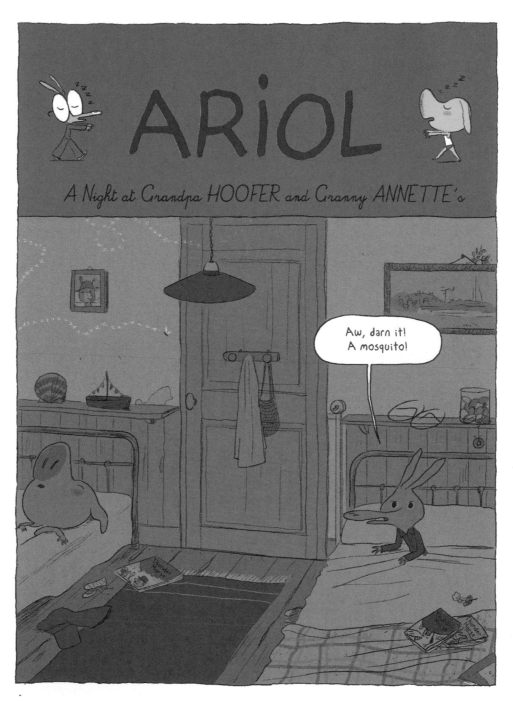

A Night at Grandpa HOOFER and Granny ANNETTE's

Hey,
RAMONO!
CLIC

RAMONO,
there's a mosquito
in the room!

WAKE UP! WE
GOTTA KILL IT!
Raaah!
He's asleep!

I'll go ask Grandpa and
Grandma if they have any
spray for mosquitoes.

BRRRZZVVVEEEE
KKRRMMPSSSSSSS
Psst!
Grandpa!
GRAANDPA!

FRRRSHLLLL
RRRSSTCHHH
Grandpa doesn't care. He's snoring and his breath stinks! That repels the mosquitoes!

KKRRROOOMMPFFF
GRRRFTSSSOOO
I don't like being all alone with a problem, 'cause that means I got to take care of it!

Oh, jeez!
I left the light on and the door open!

Now there are lots of mosquitoes! Ten at least!

Quick! Some armor!
RAMONO! WAKE-UP! We're under attack!

AAAH! Help! Leave me alone!

It's impossible to go back. I'll get bitten to death.
The best thing is to turn the light off and on in the hallway. That'll make them come out.

LATER, IN GRANDPA AND GRANNY'S ROOM...

=FFFRROOPTSSSOOO...=

Ah! Are you going to shtop shnoring, you old burro?

⇒FFFRROOPTLLLL...⇐
Hey! The light's on in the hallway! That's shtrange!

⇒BBBRRRLMMKRRRR...⇐
Maybe zhe children need shomething. I'll put my teef in sho I won't shtartle zhem.

⇒Pssst⇐ Children! Is everything okay?

They look like they're sleeping like angels. One of them must have gone to the bathroom and forgot to turn off the light afterwards.

Okay. Since I'm up and HOOFER's snoring like a buzz-saw, I'll go down and make myself a nice herbal tea.

ARFL!
Hush, REX, it's me. Don't wake everybody up. Go back to sleep.

I'll drink my tea in front of the TV, without turning on the sound. Sometimes, late at night, they show good, old murder mysteries that are a little scary. I like them.

AAAH!
AAAH!

MEANWHILE, UPSTAIRS...
AAH!
ARF! ARF!
BANG BANG
AARGH! Someone touched me!
ARF! ARF!
What's all that shouting? Do you hear that, ARIOL?

ARF! ARF!
Go get help, officer!
BANG!
ARF! ARF! ARF!
BANG!
ARIOL? ARIOL? Where are you?
ARIOL is gone!

ARF! ARF! ARF!
Down, REX!
BANG
Those crooks won't get away
BANG
ARF!
MISTER HOOFER!

ARF! ARF!
Mister HOOFER! Wake up! ARIOL and your wife are getting attacked downstairs by policemen with guns!
Mmmhuh? What? Who's that?

SOON AFTER, IN THE LIVING ROOM...

Oooh! What a fright! I almost swallowed my teeth!

That'll teach you to watch where you put your rear end!

⇒Whew!⇐
I'd have rather been bitten by mosquitoes than be crushed by Granny ANNETTE!

ARF?

I did a walk around the house. There are no bandits.
But we told you it was on TV!

Before you go to bed again, boys, go put on something warm and your shoes. I'll show you something.
You're not going to take them out at this hour?

The sun rising over the sea.

END

ARiOL
OUR COUNTY WILL, IN TURN, BE AFFECTED BY THE BIRD FLU.
Goodness me!

A pair of pigeons, Mr. and Mrs. WOODLOVE, who were returning from a trip to Asia, were hospitalized with avian flu this morning in the Ornithology Department at the Bone-Feathering Hospital.

The poor things!

What's avian flu?

LATER...
All the birds are panicking. Mrs. STERN, my swallow friend, was just on the phone. She's very worried.
I bet.

She flat out canceled her trip down south.
Eat, ARIOL.
I'm not hungry.

You have to eat, honey.
This carrot soufflé is very good.

SOON AFTER...
What's wrong with you, son? Are you sad because of those awful stories about bird flu?
Yes.

You're worried about your bird friends, is that it?
Yes.

In my class, for birds, there's KWAX, BEAKY, and MUMBELINE. And Mister RIBERA, who does our gym class, is a rooster.
I know.

I don't want KWAX to die. He's really nice.
Nobody's going to die. not KWAX nor the others. They won't even get sick, you'll see.

At this very moment, there are great scientists working to stop the illness. They'll succeed.
Tomorrow morning, we have gym with Mister RIBERA. Is it really true the flu can't pass from a rooster to a donkey?
Ptoo!

THE NEXT DAY...

All right then, kids! You're going to divide yourselves up into two groups, in fact, boys and girls together, and we'll play dodge ball!

I can't, Mister RIBERA!

Yes, it is!
They said so on TV!
And don't touch
me either!
LIAR!
♫
TWEET!

MOTHBELLA and MUMBELINE,
you two separate, in fact!
She pecked me!
Serves you
right!

We're all in perfect health here,
and there's no danger, in fact!
If there were the slightest risk, you'd
be informed. I want calm, in fact, or
I'll punish you!

PHARMAFLUFF, you'll play
just like everyone, in fact!
Otherwise, you'll be the one
getting sick, in fact. I'll talk
to your mom later!
Baaaa--

And you, KWAX, are you afraid of the bird flu?
No, on the contrary, I'd like to catch it!

When I got tonsillitis, my parents bought me a guitar. If I had the flu, they'd buy me at least a piano.
You're crazy!

That flu is super dangerous! It'll kill you!
Not ducks. My uncle's a doctor and he always says ducks are sturdy.
?

What's more, it's true. Ever since I was little, nobody has died in my family.
HEY! LOOK AT BEAKY!

OOOO!
He fell!
He's fainted!
He's dead!

HE HAS THE BIRD FLU!
?

HELP!
STAY HERE, IN FACT!
MAMA!

Heeheehee!
Gotcha, you bunch of fraidy-cats!
BEAKY!

This isn't the time to be making tasteless jokes! Go stand in the corner, in fact!
What?! I was just kidding...

Listen up, everybody! Since you and your parents are worried, in fact, by this bird flu thing, we'll have an information session at school this week!
I don't care! I won't come!

Meanwhile, we're here to do sports, in fact! So, form two teams and think only about the ball, understood?
In fact!
Pffhoohoo
Heeheehee

THE PAIR OF PASSENGER PIGEONS BELIEVED TO HAVE CONTRACTED AVIAN FLU LEFT THE HOSPITAL TODAY. MISTER AND MRS. WOODLOVE WERE ONLY SUFFERING FROM ORDINARY FOOD POISONING FROM SEAFOOD.

AAAH!

WHEW!

What did he say? Why are you happy?

HEEHAW HEEHAW HEEHAW

He said the two pigeons don't have bird flu, after all!

My phone. That must be that nice Mrs. STERN, greatly relieved!

END

ARiOL
At the TOTO Station
Are we there yet?
Not yet. I'm stopping to get gas.
FOR YOU!

I'll stay with Dad. I want to see how he gets gas.

Fine. OATS, I'll leave ARIOL with you. You two join me in the store.

Okay.

FOR YOU!

Gas stinks!
Yes, it stinks. You'd do better to go with your mother.

That thing really looks like a big pistol!
Don't come closer, ARIOL. The gas could splash on you.

How do you know the tank is full?
I know because the hose blocks up. It goes CLAK, and the gas stops flowing.
CLAK
Hey! Did you hear? It's full.

Do you want me to wash the windows?
There's a bucket here.
No thanks. Don't touch it, it's dirty. Let's go pay.
FOR YOU

Hey, Dad. I could get the big, disgusting sponge and wash your glasses with it! What do you think about that?
If you do that, I'll make you drink a quart of gas with the big pistol.

Well, I'll give you a shampoo job with gas mixed with water from the filthy bucket.
And I'll put you in the trunk, and you'll finish the trip under the suitcases.
Okay, gentlemen...

You owe me fifty-three bucks. Who's paying? The big one? The little one?
When it's expensive, Dad's always the one who pays!
Alas!

You're donkeys...
That's pretty obvious, isn't it?
I'm THUNDER HORSE!

I'm saying that because, this month, all equines buying gas at any TOTO station are eligible for gift points.
Who's eligible for a gift?
EQUINES. You and your dad, if you prefer.

ARIOL, I've explained to you a hundred times that we're EQUINES. Equines are the family of donkeys, horses, and zebras. But you know that!
What kind of gift is it?

The gentleman is a CANINE. The family of dogs, wolves, foxes...
That's right, I'm a dog! But like I always say: I don't bite! WOOFWOOFWOOFWOOF!

Equines, canines, bovines are all the same to me! We're all mammals, aren't we?
Why, of course.
Can we have our gift?

You'll get your gift once your dad has ten points. For now, I'm giving him two. And you, don't budge, I'm going to get you a little surprise.
That's nice. You don't have to, you know.
TOTO

Dad, can we get more gas? That way, the canine will give us more points.
ARIOL, come now! You don't say "canine" to talk about the gentleman!
But you're the one who called him that!

There! Till you get the big prize, the TOTO service station offers you this pretty key ring.
Great! Say thanks, ARIOL.
Thank you, sir.

All right, let's go join your Mom in the store!
OOOH! Wait!

Look what you win with ten points!
Special Offer
EQUINES
If you're a HORSE, ZEBRA, or DONKEY, Save up points AND WIN A HIPPOD!

What's a HIPPOD?
It must be that headset there, for listening to music, adapted for our ears.
THE TOTO SHOP

Hey, Mom! Dad almost won a HIPPOD!
That's nice, honey. Go pee before we leave.

I don't need to.
I know you. If you don't pee now, you'll make me stop in ten minutes. Come with me.

Dad, when will we get the HIPPOD?
Good question. Answer it yourself.

For now, I have two points. We need ten to win the HIPPOD. You get two points for every fill-up. How many points and fill-ups do we need?
Uh...

It's easy!
Yes, but I can't think and pee at the same time. Can you hold my key-ring?
Put it in your pocket.

Well? Is it coming?
Don't hurry me! It blocks my pee, if you hurry me!
No, I mean the answer to the problem. Is it coming?

Hey, you giving me problems isn't right! You're not Mister BLUNT!
It's not a problem, it's a game. A kid's game!

First, you subtract: ten points minus two points equals eight points.
I don't care, I am not listening!

Next, you divide...
Mom! I was calmly peeing, and Dad made me do math problems.
Oh! The meanie!

What do you want before we leave? Something to drink? To eat?
A pack of chewing gum!
More chewing gum!

To conclude, ARIOL, we'll have to do four more fill-ups before you get your HIPPOD.

That's too long. Will you buy me it in a store?

Towards A6

Goodbye
Till Next Ti
Drive Sa

End

ARIOL
Where Are the Keys?
160 BROADWAY
Pizzah
My keys!
What keys?

The keys to my home! They were in my pocket, now they're gone!
Did you lose them?

Look in your other pockets!
Nope!

In my backpack either!
Hurry up, we're gonna be late!

Darn it! What's more, we have a quiz on divisions this morning!
Oh, dang! I didn't study anything. I'll help you look for your keys instead.

Just tell your parents to write me a note explaining I missed class because of you.
160 BROADWAY
Yes, yes.
Promise?
Yes, I tell you! Look on the ground!

What do your keys look like?
160 BROADWAY
They're ordinary keys, with a green "TOTO" key ring.

And you didn't hear them fall?
No, and that is what's weird.
And you didn't feel the hand of the crook who took 'em from your pocket?
No.

My mom told me that, sometimes, people find keys on the street, pick them up, and leave them in a business. We'll go see in the bakery.
Good idea.

My, my! Mister ARIOL and Mister RAMONO! Not in class yet at this hour?
I lost my keys!

Did anybody give them to you, Mrs. POMPADOUR?
Oh, no, my dear.
I'd like three chocolate-caramel bears.

We could go to BEGOSSIAN's, too. We'll look at the magazines at the same time.
I don't care about magazines! I want my keys!

And do you want a bear?
RAMONO, you're not helping me! All you care about is missing school!
Leave me be. I'll look by myself!

Well, there's no use getting mad.
Yeah, I'm mad! I'm mad 'cause my dad'll have to change the locks and he's going to yank my ears.

And why would your dad change the locks? He'll get new keys made, and that's it.
Are you crazy? And the crooks?

The crooks are on the street, they see you lose your keys, they pick 'em up, they follow you to see where you live, and afterwards, they rob you! It's common knowledge!
Really?

But then, maybe they're following us right now?
Maybe. Let's run!

Stop...
I can't go on...
Let's hide under
the bus shelter!

It's not good... to run...
after eating... three
chocolate bears...
It's
all right,
we lost
'em.

Aww, jeez, I just
thought of something!
Maybe the crooks are
ALREADY at my house!
SMACK
How'd they
do that?

If they know me and know where I live, they're already doing the robbery!
We gotta call the police then.

Well, no! That's not a good idea because the police, BAM! They'll bust in your door with their shoulders.
Or with their foot, BLAM! And we'll have to change the door.

Not counting that when they come inside your house, they'll say "HANDS UP!" and they'll fire in the air, BANGBANG! to scare the crooks.
You'll have to redo the ceiling, too.

And one of the crooks, he'll surrender, but the other one will shout: "YOU WON'T GET ME!" and he'll jump behind the couch and he'll shoot like a crazy man, BANGBANGBANG!
Then we'll have to redo everything. My dad will be furious!

Let's forget the police. Come on!
Where to?
My place.

54
SLEEPY RABBIT
Your place? But you just told me the crooks are there!
Not for sure. Let's go see.

A BIT LATER...
We'll have to listen at my door. If we hear any noise, that'll mean the crooks are there.
Okay, go ahead.

We'll both go. You wanted to come with me, so come with me!
Okay, okay. Don't push.

Hey, doofus!
Look, your keys!
Ah, darn!
I'd left them
in the lock!

Whew! I'm so happy.
We'd do better to
look inside to see if
anyone came in.

It's okay.
Everything's
normal.
Get me
something to
drink. We ran,
I'm thirsty.

Okay, RAMONO, we've got to go
now. We're forty minutes late for
the divisions quiz, that's a lot.
Too bad, we
were just fine.

Well, RAMONO? What are you waiting for?

Uh... Sir, I left my backpack at ARIOL's.

END

honnnk
honk
honk
ARIOL
A Visit From Uncle PETRO
When's Uncle PETRO getting here?
ARIOL, you've asked that a hundred times! We told you he's coming for LUNCH! Change your tune!
But it's already a quarter after one!

Say, MUMULE, ARIOL's right. Your brother is late again! I'm starting to get hungry!
Have a carrot.

With all the work the poor thing has, it's understandable why he's late.
Clearly, you're always making good excuses for him!

What's all that racket in the street?
HONK HONK HONK

It's Uncle PETRO!
He's drunk to be honking like that!

HEY! RIRI! COME SEE MY NEW CAR!
Coming, Uncle!

ARIOL, stay here! You're not the one who's supposed to go down, he's supposed to come up!
I'll be back, Dad!

Well, great! Whenever your brother comes here, that boy starts champing at the bit. Once again we won't be eating on time!
Did he put a jacket on to go outside?

UNCLE PETRO!
Hey, RIRI! What's up?

You wanna drive these wheels?
Oh, yeah!
Go on, get in!

What kind of car is it?
It's called a Beta Romeo. Do you like it?
Oh, yeah!

My buddy NOONOO loaned it to me for a week. Here, just listen to this motor:
VRROOMM
Will you let me drive with you?

Say, kids, you're being good, but lunch is ready, and we're waiting for you upstairs.
Oh, hi, bro-in-law! What's up?
I'm not hungry, I want to drive!

You shouldn't have come down, we were coming up.
Who knows when!
Hey, Uncle! Want to do some judo in my bedroom?

Hey there, MUMU. What's up?
Hi, little brother.
All right, time to eat now.
SMACK
SMACK

How was your trip to Spain?
I brought back some silly gifts for you.
YAAAAAAY! PRESENTS!

Here, RIRI. I found this at the airport.
Thank your uncle, ARIOL.
A tee-shirt with Emperor MORODAN on it! SWEEEEET!

For my sis, something that smells good.
Oooo! You splurged! It's ISSEY MAKIYE!
I'm putting my tee-shirt on right away!
¡Hola ¿Qué Tal?

What happened to the bro-in-law?
Excuse me, but nobody's coming, so I'm eating!
Hola ¿Qué Tal?

Since you have everything, bro-in-law, finding you a gift isn't easy. But I brought you this back all the same.
What IS that thing?

A bull-fighting hat.
OLÉ!
HAHA! Look at Dad!
Very funny.

OH! Why that's a bowl of pistachios!
Yes. Since you were supposed to be here at noon, we'd fixed some snacks.

I know a really funny trick you can do with a bowl of pistachios.
Really?
Yes, yes, you'll see.

My friend NOONOO taught me this. Are you ready? ONE... TWO... THREE...

AND HUP!

Aw darn it! All the pistachios are on the ground!
You act surprised.
HAHAHA! Well, yeah!

Ordinarily, they should have stayed in the bowl, because of centrifugal force! It worked with NOONOO. I must not have turned my wrist fast enough.
You'll have to take the class again.

Okay then, I'll pick 'em up.
That's nice.
I'll help you, UNCLE PETRO!

ARIOL, sit down and eat!
Forget it, PETRO, we'll run the vacuum over it.
No, no, start without me. I'll nibble on this.

AFTER LUNCH...
Still want to do some judo, Uncle PETRO?
GOODNESS ME! I didn't see the time! I gotta go, buddy, I have a rendezvous!

Goodbye to the little family! See you next time! Thanks for the nice lunch!
Bye, PETRO.
Bye, Uncle.
Bye.

That sucks, I didn't even get to drive Uncle PETRO's car.
You can do so next time.

Hey, Dad? You want to do judo with me?
This hat is ridiculous.

I'm going to do a move on you.
Wait, ARIOL, get out from under my hooves, I have to run the vacuum. I see one or two--

--pistachios.

MOM! Uncle PETRO taught me a judo move and I can do it!
That's good, honey!
End

ARIOL
The Machine for Being the Best in Class
Guess what I have in my pocket.
Your hand.
Yes, besides that.

Here, look.
A pencil sharpener.

It looks like a pencil sharpener, but it's not a pencil sharpener. It's a machine that'll make me become the best in class.
It's powerful, then.

My sister's new boyfriend's invented it—BOOKRIF.
That's a funny name for a pencil sharpener.

That's not the pencil sharpener's name, doofus! It's my sister's boyfriend's name. He's super smart, not like you!
If he's smart, it's weird that he's with your sister.

Okay, FOUFAGE, you're starting to get on my nerves! Because of that, I won't show you my machine!
I don't care about your machine!

I'll only show it to ARIOL, 'cause ARIOL is my buddy! Come on, ARIOL.
Go eat your machine!

FOUFAGE isn't following us?
No. He's talking with HUBBUB and TIMBERWOLF. Go ahead, show me your thing.

You see this paper?
Yes.
I wrote this afternoon's dictation in tiny letters on it.

I roll it up, put it in the pencil-sharpener's casing while getting it to come out a little through there.
Hm.

Next, I put the sharpener in front of me and I stick a pencil into the hole. Watch closely.
Hm.

Oooo! It turns all by itself!
Yes!
RRRR...

It turns all by itself and it quietly unrolls the paper.
Not bad. What use is it?
RRRR...

Well, think: during the dictation, I set the machine behind my pencil case, I start it, and I copy the paper that's unrolling. That way, I have zero mistakes.
But won't it make noise?
RRRR...

It makes a little noise, but that's normal. BOOKRIF's motor does that.
You're going to get caught by Mister BLUNT.
RRRR...

DRRRRIIIIING
We'll just have to cough and move our chairs. That'll cover the noise.
Okay, let's go, it's time.

Hey, RAMONO! When you're best in class, I'll be the school principal!
I'm not talking to you anymore, FOUFAGE!

A BIT LATER...

Take out some paper. I'm going to see if you prepared for your dictation.

Oh, yes! I'm prepared!

Heehee!

"The next day, comma..."
Here goes.
RRRR...

"...the rain fell the whole day, period..."
KOF KOF!
Heurk! Heurk! Heurk!
CRE
CRE
CREEK
RRRR...

ARIOL and RAMONO! What's all that racket?
Uh--we swallowed down the wrong way, Mr. BLUNT
Heurk!
RRRR...

Quiet down! You're keeping the others from hearing the dictation!
That's right!
RRRR...

I'll start over.
OWWWWWW!
RRRR...

HELP! THERE'S SOMETHING IN MY HAIR!
Oh, dang!
RRR...

MOTHBELLA! QUIET!
OWWIE! RAMONO'S PULLING MY HAIR!
Darn it! Her hair got caught in the pencil sharpener!
RRPTFX...

LATER...
BOOHOOHOO!
MY HA'AA'AAI'AAIR!
I had to cut off a little, MOTHBELLA! This infernal machine was going to chew into your skull!
RRGZ..

RAMONO, you know full well you're not allowed to bring dangerous toys to class.
But it's not a toy, sir... It's my pencil sharpener!

And this little paper stuck inside... What does it say?
I-- I don't know--

"The next day... the rain... fell the whole day..."
The dictation!

Okay, class, we'll restart the dictation: "We couldn't go until the third, period."

Third period?

Hey, RAMONO! Your machine for being best in class was great!

FOUFAGE, I already told you I won't talk to you anymore

End

ARiOL
Tagging
More of that awful graffiti!
That one isn't bad.

Let's tell the watchman.
Oh, no, he'll erase it.

Mister FURRY, someone has tagged the garage door again!
I know. The third time in ten days.

It's some neighborhood kid doing it. I can't figure out who it is. Got any idea, JP?
No, Dad.

That tag is nice. We should keep it.
Don't be foolish, ARIOL.
HAHA! Copy it, if you like, but in your bedroom!

THE NEXT DAY...
⇒Psst!⇐
ARIOL!
?

You got a second?
Yes.
Follow me. I'll show you something.

Where to?
To the wall at the back of the building, behind the hedge. You know it?
Uh... not well.

Go on through.
My backpack is caught.

What do you say about that?
COOOL!

Since it's my dad who removes them, it'd drive him crazy if he found out.
What do you do them with?

With spray paint. My stuff's stashed here. Want to try?
Uh... it's just... my dad really isn't okay with this.

Nobody can see us. Here, take this.
What color is it?
Red.

And what do I do?
Well, for instance, you write a name you like. What name do you like?
THUNDER HORSE!

"THUNDER HORSE" is too long. You'd spend three hours writing it. Find something else. Something shorter.
Oh.

Aren't you in love with some girl?
Yes.
What's her name?
PETULA.

Does she know you're in love with her?
No. I don't dare tell her.
Very well. That's just what a tag is good for.

Make a cool tag and mix your initials in it. Afterwards, show it to her. It's a way to make her understand you love her. You'll see, it works.
Okay.

Here, if you like, I'll make you a model. Give me the spray paint.
Cool, thanks.

It's PETULA, you say? So first, I'll spray a big "P."
PSSSSSSSSHHH

And you're ARIOL. So, on the side, I made a big "A."

Well?
Ah! I like it!

You understand how it's done, eh? It's easy.
Yes, yes.
Next time, I'll teach you to use different colors.

Practice, if you want. I've got to go. Once you've finished, put the spray paint in the bag and the bag back in its place, okay?
Okay.

Bye, ARIOL!
Bye, JP! And thanks, eh?

Okay then... my turn.

THE NEXT DAY, AFTER SCHOOL...
PETULA? If you have five minutes, I'd like to show you something secret.
What is it?

It's a hiding place where I've hidden a treasure.
What kind of treasure?
You'll see.

Come on through.
Ouch! My hair!

So now, you have to close your eyes and give me your hand.
It's not a joke, is it?
No, no. Don't be afraid.

IDIOT! All that to tell me you love your dad?

No, wait, let me explain--

End

ARIOL
DONG!
HOOFER, drop me off for five minutes at the church. I have to talk to the priest.
Alrighty then! We'll be here an hour at least! We'll wait for you at the bistro. Eh, boys?
No. We want to go with granny.

Are you sure you don't want some ice-cold lemonade?
Afterwards. I'll show RAMONO the church first.

I'd rather go to the bistro. I'm thirsty.
Wait, you'll see. You'll like it.

Children, I must have a quick talk with Father BRILLET about the choir, so behave in the church, and don't make any noise.
Okay.

What's a "choir"?
My grandma sings in a group. Come on, I'll show you something.

Does she do recordings with her group?
We'll go this way.

Aw dang! It's closed!
We'll go to the bistro then.

Usually, this is called the crypt and there are candles and a kind of little window, where they put a piece of SAINT AMPOIRE's skeleton.
I don't see it.

I'll ask Father BRILLET if he'll open it for us.
I'd rather go to the bistro.

Do you know what that is?
No.
It's a confessional.
What's it for?

You'll see. Go in that way, I'll go this way.
Okay.

Another grate!
It's for talking through. We have to tell secrets.

Well, my secret is that you're as blind as a bat.
And my secret is that your snout stinks.
PFFFHEEHEEHEE!

We're having fun, eh?
And where does this door go?

A stairwell.
Wait. My granny said we were to stay in the church.

We're just taking a look.
A quick one, then.

WHEW!
There are lots of steps!
It's because... we're... in the bell tower...

Look. Some kind of... machine thing.

Here's where the crows live.

A ladder.
I wanna see.
Let's go back now.
It's dangerous.

WOW! COOOOL!
What?

Huge bells!
Oh, yeah.

You know what? The thing down below must be for ringing them.
We're almost there. ATTACK!

YEEAAHH! We're the conquerors of Emperor MORODAN's castle!
The sun hurts my eyes!

Whoa! We're super high up!
You see the whole village.

Hey, isn't that your granny down there coming out of the church?
Oh, yes, darn!

We have to call her, or else they'll leave without us! GRAAANNY!
GRAAANY!

GRAAAANNY!
She doesn't hear. She's as deaf as your grandpa.

Wait! I have an idea!
Where are you going?

HOOFER, the kids aren't with you?
No, since they're with you!

DONG! DONG

Stop, RAMONO!

If they don't hear us now, their ears really are plugged up!

END

ARIOL
DISCO QUEEN
Do you know what this is, ARIOL?
No.
It's my record player from when I was twelve. It's for listening to records!
ANNIE

I thought it was gone and I just found it by chance in the back of the front closet. I'm really happy.
⇒PFFFFFF!!⇐
Does it work?
ANNIE

We'll see. I've kept a few old records in my bedroom. We'll try them.
Will you give it to me, if it does?

So, let's see if I still know how to use it. First, we plug it in...
It looks like something for making crepes.

Next, we lift the arm and, ordinarily, that makes the platter turn.
YEAH! It's turning! Quick, put on a record!

Hoho! I haven't opened this box of records in at least ten years!
Will you make me some crepes, mom?

"Pop is Pop" by HOOTER and NUTJOB! COOL! A huge hit! Here, we'll put it on!
Your record is all black!

This is called a 45, with a song on each side.
That's not many.
Look, I set the needle down geeently...

♫ BING BONG CRRR... DJWEEEE FLUNK CRR... ♫ CRRR...
Here we go! Are you dancing, ARIOL?
YEAH!

♫ TROOT
BLURP
GRUNK
CRRR...
FWEEEEEF!
CRRR...♫
My old machine still works. Come on! Let's party! Get down!
Totally!

♫ CRRRpop!
VOOzzzz
PopCRRRR...
TAGADAP!
CRRR...♫
There's a special dance for this song. First, you lay your ears flat, your hands like this, and you bend your knees.
The record's a little scratchy.

♫ Pop!
Woga
Woga
CRRR...
Pop!
CRRR...♫
CRRR...
Next, your ears and left arm in the air, pointing your finger.
Your LEFT arm, ARIOL.
Oh, yes.

♫ Pop Is
Pop!
CRRR...
SCHWING
SCHWING
YEAH!
CRRR...♫
And then, on the refrain, you make a good kick to the rear while singing "POP IS POP!"
What does that mean?
Nothing, it's just a dumb refrain.

KREEK
PLOOTS
POP!
FAFL
CRRR...
POPIZPOP!
That's good, honey! You dance like a pro!

Popisbam
Popisbam
Popisbam
Popisbam
What's wrong with the record?
It's scratched, it's too bad. It was played too much! We'll put on another one.

In the meantime, I'm going to dress up as THUNDER HORSE! It'll be more like a party!
Okay. Good idea.

I'll also take my magic lasso. That's good for dancing.

TATATA! Here's THUNDER HORSE who wants to do a MEGA DANCE PARTY!

WOOW! You look really pretty!
Of course, I made an effort to dance with THUNDER HORSE.

Okay, now let's see... What do we put on this time?
Something I can dance to with my magic lasso!

THIS!
OH!

Well, what?
Is it no good?
Uh... yes, yes, it's very good, but it's very slow. It doesn't get you moving. Something else would be better.

I don't care, I want to try it. I like the cover.
Okay, we'll try.

Will you show me how to dance?
♫ CRRR... CRRR... CRRR...

HEY! MOM! WILL YOU SHOW ME HOW TO DANCE?
♫ CRRR... CRRR... CRRR...
Sniff!

♫ CRRR... CRRR...
Well, what's wrong with you? Why are you sad?
It's nothing, it's nothing... I'm not sad...

Here, look, it's easy. We hold each other like this...
♫ CRRR... CRRR... ♫
Why are you crying? I don't want you to cry!

And then we turn, slowly, gently--
♫ CRRR... CRRR... ♫
You've stopped crying, eh?

Yes, I've stopped, honey. It's just that music brought back an old memory to me...
♫ CRRR... CRRR... ♫
I'm not a honey, I'm THUNDER HORSE and I don't want you to be sad.

What's the memory of?
CRRR...
CRRR...
It's dumb. It's when I was thirteen. I was in love with a mule named BADIM.

What's a MULE?
A half-breed. His mama was a donkey and his daddy a horse.
CRRR...
CRRR...
Lucky guy!
He was very handsome.

But one day, at a party, this music was playing and he danced with another girl, and I saw him give her a kiss. It made me jealous.
CRRR...
CRRR...
And where was Dad?

Oh, I didn't know your daddy yet! I met him a long time afterwards. I was little back then.
CRRR...
CRRR...
CRRR...
Okay, we'll change records then.

♫ DISCO QUEEN ♫

♫ DISCO QUEEN, YOU ARE MY DISCO QUEEN!! ♫

Heeheehee

WOOSH! WOOSH! YAAA!

End

ARiOL
Fleas
Come on, HUBBUB! Do you think you'll find the answer to the problem easier by scratching yourself?
It's not that, sir. I'm scratching because it's itchy...
45
x 5

You haven't gotten fleas, I hope?
I don't know, sir. I hope not.
45
x 5
SCRATCH SCRATCH

⇒Pssst!⇐ We'll say we're itchy, too. That way, maybe Mr. BLUNT will send us home.
Oh, yeah! Good one!

Sir! Sir! I'm itchy, too!
And me, too, sir! I feel lots of bugs crawling on me!

ARIOL and RAMONO! Settle down! Don't try to take advantage of the situation, eh?
AAAH!

Sir! I'm itchy!

Me, too sir!

Can I scratch myself, sir?

Me, too!

Do fleas make you sick?

CALAMITY, sit back down! You others, Quiet! Don't make me bark!

Sir! Do you have fleas, too?
Uh... I... hmm. I have been a little itchy for a moment or two. But there's no use getting upset!
SCRATCH SCRATCH

ARIOL, instead of acting like an idiot with RAMONO, go with HUBBUB to see the nurse and ask Mrs. LATIFA to examine the two of you. Now get jumping!
Yes, sir.
SCRATCH SCRATCH

Do you really have fleas?
Well, I don't know. It's just itchy.

By faking scratching, I've gotten itchy for real.
RMARY
By the way, do you know how much 45 times 5 is?
BEFORE ENTERIN

Mrs. LATIFA!
You should knock before coming in, kid!
We have fleas.
SCRATCH SCRATCH
SCRATCH SCRATCH

He started it!
No, it was him!
TUT TUT! Don't be arguing!
SCRATCH SCRATCH
SCRATCH SCRATCH

Where are you itching?
Uh... on my legs.
Drop your pants, please.
No way!

I don't want to drop my pants! I was wrong, it's my arms that are itchy!
DROP YOUR PANTS, I said! And don't argue, I have to examine you.

We don't joke around with fleas at school, do you understand? Turn around.
♫ ⇒Pffrrt⇐ ARIOL, we see your undies! ♫
Very nice, eh?

Okay. No fleas or any sign of fleas. Let's see your torso now.
♫ Your undies are gre-en
You're stupid, HUBBUB!

Nothing at all. No fleas. Next.
I'm not itchy anymore. It's over. I feel all right. By the way, do you know how much 45 times 5 is?

Raise your sweater so I can see you.
But I told you nothing's wrong!
Heh heh!

AH! You, on the other hand, are a little red!
It's because I scratched myself!
WHOAAA! YUCK!

Take your sweater all the way off, so I can see better.
NOOO! I DON'T WANT TO!
Get naked, HUBBUB!

HELP! YOU'RE STRANGLING ME! ARGL!
Well, what's stuck?
Can I help you pull, Mrs. LATIFA?

You have a collar inside of your turtle neck?
SNIFF!
A collar? Show me!

A flea collar, in fact!
My- my mom made me wear it... ->SNIFF!<-
HA HAHA!

Stop laughing, you! It's not funny!
He was making fun of me just now!
->RNIFL!<-

Your mama is right. Those collars work. They protect you.
Yes, but I wanted a bracelet, one with spikes. A collar is girly.

So, I have to wear turtlenecks to hide it and afterwards, if I have to do multiplications on the board, I get hot and my sweater is itchy. SNIFF!
Okay, okay, I understand. Blow your nose. Your snout is runny.

In any case, the good news is that you don't have fleas. And if you want, I'll talk to your mama about your collar, okay?
HONK!
I'm thirsty, Mrs. LATIFA.

Go drink from the sink, and afterwards, back to class with you!

I warn you, if you tell the others I have a flea collar, I'll tell them you have green undies.
So what? Green undies are very pretty.

I'll walk you back.
You won't say anything about my collar, eh?
Whoa the ♫ girl-uh ♫

Uh... don't come in, Mrs. LATIFA. We thought we saw a flea on the ground...

End

ARIOL
CLIK CLIK
Smile!
Children, here's Mister BERVILLE, who's going to take our class photo.
Hello, everyone.
HELLO, SIR!
Hello, ma'am!
Heehee!

Before doing the group photo, in the courtyard, Mister BERVILLE will photograph you one by one.
Sir?

Can you photograph us one by one together?
We wanna be in the same picture.

You'll be in the same picture later. For now, each one takes a turn in alphabetical order. ARIOL, you start.
Come on, kid.

It seems like you and your pal are good buddies.
Well, yeah. He's my buddy.

So, here's my little studio. Have a seat.
Why did you set up umbrellas?

What do you mean a different one? You want the photo of your pig buddy?
No, I want PETULA's picture.

PETULA is the little curly-haired cow with freckles and a tee-shirt...
Be quiet for a second, please. Look at me and smile.

CLICK
There. That's very good.

You send the next person now.
You'll remember, eh? PE-TU-LA. You'll save me her pic, but don't tell her.

I bet he won't do it!

Next.
BATTLEMESS isn't here. It's BIZZBILLA's turn. Go ahead, BIZZBILLA.
Yes.

Uh... hello.
Come in, kid. Come sit here.

You're an inch or so too short. Don't move. We got it covered.
Say...

HUP! A flick of the wrist and it rises by itself.
Can I see the photo of ARIOL?
Who's photo?

ARIOL... He's the little donkey who went before me.
AAAH! But for goodness' sake, why are you all asking me for someone else's photo?

ARIOL asked you for a picture?
Yes, he wants the picture of some girl--
BIZZBILLA?

No, not BIZZBILLA. I forget. A little goat with pigtails, I think.
POF
PETULA?
Yes, that's it, PETULA.

Okay. Look at me and smile, please.
SNIFF!

BOOHOOHOOHOO!
Ohhhhh! What's wrong with you?

I can't do your portrait, if you're crying!
I don't care! I'm uuuugly!
No way, you're not ugly!

You're sad because of the little donkey? You like the little donkey?
Yes, sniff.
You poor, little gal!

You know what? Since he asked me for a photo, I'll give him yours.
He doesn't want my photo! He wants PETULA's.
Not at all.

We'll make such a pretty picture, he'll want to keep it forever. But for that, you have to stop crying and give me your prettiest smile. Okay?
Okay.

CLICK
Perfect.

And will you give me ARIOL's picture?
Ah, not right away! I have to print it for you first. You'll have it by the end of the morning.

LATER...
Okay, kids, get in place for the group photo!
Hey, sir!

Did you think about what I said to you?
Ah, yes. Here, it's in this envelope.
Sweet.

And me, sir?
For you, it's this envelope here. Quickly go sit in front.
Thanks bunches.

Are you ready, kids? I'll count to three. ONE...

TWO...
DARN IT! HE MESSED UP!

...THREE! And I only want to see big smiles!
CLICK

END

ARiOL
No Luck, ARIOL!
OWW!

Are you okay, ARIOL? Did you get hurt?
OwwOwwOww OUCH!

HEY, GUYS! ARIOL GOT HURT!
OOO! Jeez! Jeez owwowwowwoww! Oww!

STOP A MINUTE, OKAY?
OOOOH! I'm bleeding!

Lemme see?
CAREFUL! DON'T TOUCH!

It's not dirty. I only blew my nose once.

DON'T TOUCH, I SAID!

Why did you stop playing?

ARIOL's bleeding.

Where?

His knee.

You're the one who made me fall, TIMBERWOLF! It's your fault!
Whoa! You tripped over your ears which were dragging on the ground!

All right, come on, guys! Let's continue the game.
I'll never play soccer with you again!

Okay. Are you getting back up?
Help me.

OWW!
Is your leg broken?
I don't know. It burns.

Take me back home. I can't walk by myself.
♫ PIN POM PIN POM, Home you go with RAMONO. ♫

To go faster, we'll totally get there by helicopter. FLAP FLAP FLAP FLAP FLAP
I don't care. I'm going to tell my dad TIMBERWOLF pushed me.

What happened to you, ARIOL?
Uh... nothing.
He fell during soccer.

But you're bleeding.
Barely.
Hey, BIZZBILLA! You want to give him mouth-to-mouth?

Go ahead, lean on me.
No, no, I promise you it's nothing.
Hey, BIZBILLA. You want to give him mouth-to-mouth?

Shut up, idiot! Don't you see he's hurt?
BUT I TOLD YOU I'M OKAY!
She's i-i-n-n lo-ove!

What are you three up to?
Did you fall, ARIOL?
No, I didn't fall.
TIMBERWOLF pushed him.

TIMBERWOLF didn't push me!
TIMBERWOLF is good at soccer.
Make up your mind.

It wasn't TIMBERWOLF. I slipped.
In any case, you're bleeding!
Go get your mom to take care of you.

I DON'T NEED MY MOM! I CAN BLEED BY MYSELF! Uh... TAKE CARE of myself!
Come on, ARIOL!

LEAVE ME ALONE! I'M GOING TO PUT MY KNEE UNDER THE FAUCET, AND THAT'S IT!
Okay then.

His leg was broken two minutes ago, and now he's running.

?
POW

HAVE YOU GONE CRAZY?
That was for "mouth-to-mouth!"

BIZBILLA gave me a big kick in the butt.
Good job.

You ready? You still wanna go home?
No. Let's go back to soccer.

Well? Your scrape?
It hurts a lot, but I don't care. I'm going to play anyways.

♫ THUNDER HOOORSE-- ♫
Hey, ARIOL!

♫ HE'S GOING TO PLAY SOOOCCERRR... ♫
Be careful, you didn't retie your shoelace.

Okay. This time we're going home.

END.

WATCH OUT FOR PAPERCUTZ

Welcome to the fourth, fuzzy, fantabulous ARIOL graphic novel, by the super-talented team of Emmanuel Guibert and Marc Boutavant, from Papercutz, those homo-sapiens dedicated to publishing great graphic novels for all ages. I'm Jim Salicrup, Editor-in-Chief and Thunder Horse's third biggest fan, and I'm here to recount a recent encounter of the ARIOL-kind.

Last year, none other than ARIOL artist, Marc Boutavant, paid a visit to the United States of America, appearing at such places as the New York Public Library, the Museum Of Modern Art Design Store, and The Miami Book Fair. Everywhere he went he spoke about ARIOL signed, ARIOL graphic novels, and even drew sketches in ARIOL graphic novels. But one of the most exciting stops of Marc's New York adventure was a special signing at Brooklyn's Bergen Street Comics, for it was there that I kind of finally met the entire ARIOL creative team. While Marc was there in-person, Emmanuel Guibert appeared live from France via Skype. Here's a pic of all three of us:

Both Emmanuel and Marc are as delightful as you'd probably imagine the creators of ARIOL to be, if not even more so. Together they answered questions, shared behind-the-scenes stories, and explained how they work together writing and drawing each ARIOL graphic novel. Everyone in attendance had a fun time, and I can't wait to see the two of them again! It was almost like meeting Ariol and Ramono in person!

I also can't wait for ARIOL #5 "Bizzbilla Hits the Bullseye," coming soon! Don't miss it!

Thanks,

Jim

STAY IN TOUCH!

EMAIL: salicrup@papercutz.com
WEB: www.papercutz.com
TWITTER: @papercutzgn
FACEBOOK: PAPERCUTZGRAPHICNOVELS
REGULAR MAIL: Papercutz, 160 Broadway, Suite 700, East Wing, New York, NY 10038

Other Great Titles From PAPERCUTZ™